OSCAR'S
AMERICAN DREAM

written by
BARRY WITTENSTEIN

illustrated by
KRISTEN & KEVIN HOWDESHELL

schwartz & wade books · new york

Oskar Nowicki
arrived at Ellis Island
carrying his life in a cardboard suitcase
and a skinny roll of money in his coat pocket,
a loan from his mother in Poland
for a down payment on his dream.

A barbershop.

On New Year's Eve 1899,
Oskar replaced the *k* in his name with a *c*
and celebrated a new century
with the grand opening of Oscar's All-American Barbershop
on the corner of Front Street and Second Avenue.

Oscar gave free haircuts
to the first twenty gentleman customers
and lemon drops to all the boys and girls.
It was his way of giving back.

When Oscar married in 1908,
he traded in his smock for a subway conductor's uniform.
The job paid better.

Front St

2nd Av

Out went the mirrors, shaving lotion, brushes, and razors.

In moved Out with the Old,

a women's clothing store with bargain-basement prices.

New owners Nettie and Yettie Jaffe
had a close-up view in 1915
of the suffragettes parading past their window.
Finally, a woman's right to vote felt so close
they could practically touch it.

In the early 1920s,
the sisters got rich selling the newest rage,
flapper and Jazz Age fashions.
The good times were here to stay—

until the stock market crashed,
and millions like Nettie and Yettie lost everything.
The Great Depression grabbed the nation by the throat
and would not let go.
Starting on Black Tuesday, October 29, 1929,
the Roaring Twenties
Roared. No. More.

That's when Sacred Souls and Saints heard the cries
and came to the rescue,
opening its soup kitchen and its heart.

In came ovens and tables, pots and pans, spoons and ladles.
Every day, hundreds of men, women, and children were fed.
No one was ever turned away.

During World War II,
posters of Uncle Sam hung from the walls,
"God Bless America" played on the radio,
and army recruiters appeared with big smiles
and strong handshakes.
Young men lined up around the block,
eager for the chance to become heroes.
That's what patriotism looked like in 1941.

Four years later,
the soldiers returned victorious and
married their high school sweethearts,
then fled the city for fresh air and green grass.

In their place, a new wave arrived,
this time from the air.
Moises Ortiz Jr. landed,
carrying his life in a cardboard suitcase
and a skinny roll of money in his pocket,
a loan from his brother in Puerto Rico.
He saw an opportunity.

As he walked down Front Street,
Moises came upon a boarded-up building
with a barber's pole outside,
a torn poster of Uncle Sam inside,
and a window stencil that read
"Every soul is sacred."
He had an idea.

Front St

2nd Ave

I WANT YO
FOR U.S. ARM

Every Soul
is Sacred

A bodega.

For two years,
Bodega Suprema sold everything
from cigars to coffee beans, toilet paper to newspapers,
and foods from home,
like green banana cakes and guava preserves.

But not televisions.

Which gave Moises
another idea.

Down came the Caribbean spices,
and up went wooden boxes with glass screens,
black-and-white images flickering across them.
Bodega Suprema became Renate's TV Center,
named after Moises's baby girl.

It was a huge success.
On September 23, 1960,
Moises kept the store open late
so passersby could witness history—
the first presidential debate ever shown on TV,
between John F. Kennedy and Richard Nixon.

Moises always said he loved America
because the only constant was change . . .

. . . until one night, change came knocking.
In a flash, Moises's dreams were *no más.*

Children rode by on their bicycles
to peek in at the store's charred remains,
and dared each other to run through
before the ceiling came crashing down.

But the proud corner store kept standing.

In the summer of 1963,
peaceful protestors fueled up
at Annie & Danny's Coffee Shop,
then headed off to Washington, DC,
to hear Martin Luther King Jr.

MARCH ON WASHINGTON

EQUAL RIGHTS FOR ALL!

And so it continued.

A local news reporter wrote that
if you wanted to see American history,

you just stood in the doorway
of the corner store,
and history came to you.

Then, on New Year's Eve 1999, history ended.

Candy's Homemade Old-Tyme Candies posted a poem

to its customers:

"Sometimes life is sour,

sometimes life is sweet.

Our memories of you will always be the sweetest."

OUT WITH THE OLD, IN WITH NEW
LUXURY APARTMENTS THAT KISS THE CLOUDS!

Front St

2nd Ave

ACME CONSTRUCTION

Coming Soon

Luxury Apartment Homes

From 1 to 3 bedroom apartments
with terraces.

And Acme Construction put up a billboard.

"Out with the old, in with new luxury apartments that kiss the clouds!"

SOMETIMES LIFE IS SOUR,
SOMETIMES LIFE IS SWEET.

OUR MEMORIES OF YOU
WILL ALWAYS BE
THE SWEETEST.

Candy

CANDY'S
BED | RARE CANDIES

CLOSED

CANDY'S
OLD-TYME CANDIES

CLOSED

SOMETIMES LIFE IS SOUR,
SOMETIMES LIFE IS SWEET.

OUR MEMORIES OF YOU
WILL ALWAYS BE
THE SWEETEST.

Candy

SAVE
CANDY'S

SAVE
CANDY'S

On the morning the bulldozers arrived,
a small crowd gathered,
hoping to stop the "wheels of progress."

A young woman watched from across the street,
then came over and introduced herself to everyone.

"I'm Jasmin Nowicki," she said,
and took out a photo of a man standing in that exact spot
one hundred years earlier.
"This is my great-grandfather Oscar."

No one recognized the man in the picture.

No one
except an old woman in a wheelchair.
She touched Jasmin's arm.
"It's personal for me, too," she whispered.

"Why is that?" Jasmine asked.

The old woman handed her a small brown bag.
"Would you like a lemon drop?"

Oscar Nowicki 1899

AUTHOR'S NOTE

History is more than a subject in a book. Did you ever think you could better understand the past by looking at just one building? That's what I tried to do in *Oscar's American Dream*. Though the story I've written is fictional, corner stores like this one could be found all over twentieth-century America, transforming themselves through the years along with our growing, changing nation.

Here is some historical background about the key events described in the book:

From the late 1880s to the 1920s, millions of immigrants from non-English-speaking countries in Europe, like Poland, Italy, and Russia, arrived at Ellis Island in New York Harbor. It was their dream—their American Dream—to make a better life for themselves and their families.

In 1848, the fight for women's voting rights was born in Seneca Falls, New York, when Elizabeth Cady Stanton wrote the first Declaration of Rights and Sentiments. Then, in 1919, after almost eighty years of protest, the Nineteenth Amendment to the US Constitution passed. Women finally won the right to vote.

Beginning in 1920, an era known as the Roaring Twenties, many people had factory jobs making mass-produced items like automobiles and home appliances. There was money to spend and there were items to spend it on. Young women called flappers embraced the new spirit of freedom and danced the nights away in their fringy fashions. For the first time, more Americans lived in cities than on farms.

Unfortunately, those rowdy, rip-roaring times didn't last. In 1929, the stock market crashed, and almost everyone's savings disappeared overnight when the banks closed. People lost their homes and businesses. Families went hungry. This began the Great Depression.

For ten years, there was no work and no money. Small shops like the one in this story became free food kitchens, serving up soup, bread, and other food to people struggling to get back on their feet.

By 1939, World War II had begun, and in 1941, Japan bombed Pearl Harbor in Hawaii. The United States entered the war. Young men and women flocked to recruitment centers, where they signed up to become soldiers and fight for their country. Factories hung Help Wanted signs. It wasn't long before most Americans had jobs, money, and food again. The Great Depression was over.

After the United States defeated Japan and Germany in 1945, victorious soldiers returned home. But they didn't want to raise their families in cramped apartments in the city. They married, bought cars, and headed elsewhere for homes of their own. This was the growth of suburbia—areas with green grass, fresh air, and wide-open spaces within a short drive from large cities.

The popularity of televisions in the 1950s changed family life, entertainment, and politics, as well as how people received daily news. People sat close to the small screen of flickering black-and-white images, which connected the nation and the events of the world in a way that had never been imagined. When the first-ever presidential debate took place in 1960, between Richard Nixon and John F. Kennedy, those who listened on the radio thought Nixon had won. But those who watched it on TV believed Kennedy was the clear winner. Such was the power of television.

During this time, the civil rights movement was in full force. In 1963, 250,000 peaceful protesters traveled to the March on Washington. There, they witnessed Dr. Martin Luther King Jr. give his "I Have a Dream" speech. A year later, in 1964, the Civil Rights Act passed, ending segregation—the separation of white and black people in public places.

Yes, history is much more than a subject in a book. It is alive. And if you stand on a corner and look carefully, you might even see it go marching by.